WHO WILL
LEAD KIDDUSH?

❖ ❖ ❖

WHO WILL LEAD KIDDUSH?

by Barbara Pomerantz
illustrated by Donna Ruff

❖ ❖ ❖

Union of American Hebrew Congregations
New York, New York

Publication of this book was made possible
by a generous grant from the
AUDRE AND BERNARD RAPOPORT
Library Fund

To Sherwin
who makes every day
as special as Shabbat

When young children are confronted by the divorce of their parents, they are often frightened, bewildered, and angry—frightened because they do not know how much life is going to change, bewildered because they do not understand how and why this happened, angry because they do not want life to be altered in the ways divorce demands.

Within the context of Judaism there are traditions and rituals which can continue to add stability and predictability to an unstable and often unpredictable new arrangement. Young children can count on *Shabbat*. It always comes; and with it comes the chanting of the *Kiddush*, which can be carried on regardless of the restructuring of the family. This is just one of the many constants in Judaism. The Chanukah candles still can be kindled. The Purim costume still can be worn.

It is important for children and their parents to know that some things need never change. Among them are the traditions of holiday celebrations and life-cycle events, which can continue in a one-parent home as well as in a home where the total family unit remains intact. Though a marriage may end, the *mitzvot* associated with it, such as parents teaching children and children honoring parents, do not. It may be more difficult to transmit the values of our religion to youngsters in a home where there has been divorce, but it is possible to meet this challenge if we understand that Judaism can be an ongoing, ever-present source of continuity in our lives.

Tonight, it is my turn to lead *Kiddush* with Mommy. I will sing the words Mommy and Daddy taught me when I was little. I will say *"Shabbat shalom"* to Mommy. She will say *"Shabbat shalom"* to me.

When Daddy lived here, he used to lead *Kid-dush*. I would take the heavy, silver *kiddush* cup from its special place in the cabinet.

"This cup belonged to your great-grandfather," Daddy would say. Then he would pour sweet, red wine into it.

We would all sing the special prayer together. Daddy would take a drink of wine and pass the cup to Mommy. She would take a drink and pass the cup to me.

That was when Daddy lived here.

A few months ago, before Daddy moved to his new apartment, I was in his bedroom. He was putting his books into a big box. I was feeling very sad.

Daddy came over and sat on the bed with me. "Debby," he said, "I promise we will talk on the phone every evening. We will be together on Sundays and Wednesdays and some Fridays."

"But, if you go away, who will read to me?" I asked.

"Mommy reads you bedtime stories. But, if you have a favorite book you want to read, you can save it for the times we will be together." Daddy put his tool chest on the chair.

"But, if you go away, who will build the *sukah*?"
I asked.

"I will come and build the walls and roof. Joshie next door can help you with the decorations as he does every year. And, when I come to see you, we can have dinner together in our *sukah*," Daddy said.

"With Mommy, too?" I asked.

"Mommy can eat with us if she wants to. It will be her *sukah* also," Daddy answered as he put the shiny, silver cup into the box.

"But, if you go away, who will lead *Kiddush*?" I asked. I closed my eyes to keep in the tears. But that didn't work. Daddy gave me his handkerchief and put his arm around me.

"I want you to be here every Friday night just as you've always been," I cried.

"That can't happen, Debby," Daddy said. "But I will tell you what can happen." He led me to his desk and took a calendar from the drawer. With a red pen he drew a circle around all the Fridays on the calendar. Then he put an M in one circle and a D in the next and an M in the next and a D in the next.

"Now," Daddy said, "when there is an M for Mommy in the circle, that Friday night you and Mommy will lead *Kiddush* together." Then he pointed to the next circle. "The D in the circle is for Daddy," he said. "That Friday night you and I will lead *Kiddush* together, and, if you want to, you can sleep at my apartment." Daddy held me close to him.

"You're going to share me?" I put my hand in Daddy's.

"Yes," he answered, and he kissed my fingers.

"It will be easier to share me if you stay here," I said.

"I know," Daddy answered. "But, even though some weeks we won't be in the same place, I will say *Kiddush* and you will say *Kiddush*. And we will think about each other."

"But I don't know all the words to *Kiddush,* so you'll have to stay."

"Debby, Mommy and I will help you," Daddy said.

"But Mommy and I are girls. Girls don't lead *Kiddush,* so you'll have to stay."

"Girls can lead *Kiddush* just like boys." Daddy answered.

It made me very sad to think about *Shabbat* without Daddy, or *Shabbat* without Mommy. I wanted the three of us to be together, always.

"But you put the *kiddush* cup into the box," I said. "If you go away, what will I use to lead *Kiddush*?" I felt so mad; I ran out of Daddy's room and locked my bedroom door. I wouldn't come out even when Mommy called me for dinner.

When Daddy finished packing, he asked me to open my door, but I wanted him to know I was very, very mad, so I stayed locked in. He said, "I love you Debby. I will call you tomorrow night. I promise." I heard him talking to Mommy. Then he went out the front door.

Daddy kept his promise. He did call me the next night. He asked me to come to his new apartment for *Shabbat*. Daddy picked me up in his car on

Friday afternoon. I put my overnight case into the back seat and waved good-bye to Mommy. She was standing by the door. She blew me a kiss. I blew her two—one for the night and one for the morning.

When we got to Daddy's apartment, he showed me where I would sleep. It was a sofa that opened into a bed. On the sofa there was a package wrapped in yellow paper. Daddy said the package was for me. I tore off the paper. Inside the small box was a shiny, silver cup. I ran to my Daddy and hugged him as hard as I could. Daddy bent down and looked at me right in my eyes as if I were a mirror.

"Debby," he said, "this *kiddush* cup is exactly like the one my grandpa gave me for my Bar Mitzvah when I was thirteen." He put my hair behind my ears the way he always does and said, "I know you're a long way from thirteen, but I decided you need this cup now. I love you Debby, and I will never stop, no matter how many Friday nights go by."

I felt very grown up. I decided to keep my *kiddush* cup in the same cabinet where Daddy used to keep his. Now, when Mommy and I lead *Kiddush,* I will have a beautiful, silver cup to hold. And when Daddy and I lead *Kiddush,* I will have a beautiful, silver cup to hold.

Tonight, it is my turn to lead *Kiddush* with Mommy. I will sing the words Mommy and Daddy taught me when I was little. I will say *"Shabbat shalom"* to Mommy. She will say *"Shabbat shalom"* to me. And, even though I still wish Daddy were here, I know he also will be saying *Kiddush* tonight. We will be thinking about each other.

About the Author

Barbara Rashbaum Pomerantz was involved in Jewish early childhood education for thirteen years before making aliyah in 1984. Her book *Bubby, Me, and Memories* (UAHC) was presented the Kenneth B. Smilen/Present Tense literary award and the Association of Jewish Libraries award in 1983. Mrs. Pomerantz lives in Jerusalem with her husband, Sherwin, and teenage daughter, Deborah.

About the Artist

Donna Ruff is a free-lance illustrator whose other books include *Our Golda: The Story of Golda Meir* and *Eleanor Roosevelt: First Lady of the World* for Viking Press, and *The Chanukah of Great Uncle Otto* for the Jewish Publication Society. She has won several awards for her illustration and film animation. She and her family live in New York City.